A TASTE FOR
VICTORY

D0649330

STONE ARCH BOOKS
a capstone imprint

JAKE MADDOX
GRAPHIC NOVELS

Published by Stone Arch Books,
an imprint of Capstone.
1710 Roe Crest Drive
North Mankato, Minnesota 56003
www.capstonepub.com

Library of Congress Cataloging-in-Publication Data
is available on the Library of Congress website.

ISBN: 978-1-4965-9714-4 (library binding)
ISBN: 978-1-4965-9924-7 (paperback)
ISBN: 978-1-4965-9759-5 (ebook PDF)

Summary: Hank Watson loves playing basketball
and helping his team win big games. But he has
another passion too—cooking! When Hank has an
opportunity to meet celebrity chef Brenton Spooner,
he jumps at the chance. But while practicing a
difficult dish, he accidentally burns his hand. The
injury affects his performance both on the court and
in the kitchen. Will Hank come through in the clutch
and help his team win the big game and still impress
his cooking hero?

Editor: Aaron Sautter
Designer: Cynthia Della-Rovere
Production Specialist: Tori Abraham

Printed in the United States of America.
PA117

A TASTE FOR VICTORY

Text by Brandon Terrell
Art by Berenice Muñiz
Color by Armando Ramirez
Lettering by Jaymes Reed

COACH ROGERS

BRENTON SPOONER

Kidz COOK

CHARLIE BEST

7

Both basketball and cooking need certain elements for success.

Abdi, set a pick for Hank, and Hank, you take it to the hoop.

First, you need a recipe. Like Coach Rogers's playbook . . .

WHUMP!

. . . or the recipe book gramma left me when she died.

Without a gameplan, you don't know if you'll be tasting sweet victory or bitter defeat.

11

—legendary chef (and my culinary hero), Brenton Spooner.

SPAGHETTI ALLA CARBONARA

BRENTON SPOONER

Come on now, Sadie! There's only five minutes left to finish your dish!

Spooner hosted KidzCook, a cooking competition show. I'd actually sent in an audition tape to be a contestant but hadn't heard back.

Kidz COOK

In order to keep myself from obsessing about the audition, I spent my time either on the court or in the kitchen.

13

14

Yep. Just the three of us tonight. Smells delicious as usual, champ.

That night, when I walked into the dining room, I saw the stack of mail . . . and the letter.

Kidz COOK

Hank Watson
202 Oak Ridge Lane
Indianapolis, Indiana, 47304

The letter that could change everything.

I'd done it.

I'd earned a chance to cook a meal for my idol.

If all went well, I'd make it onto the show.

Needless to say, I was jazzed the next day.

The excitement stayed with me. Whatever came my way . . .

WHHMP!

. . . I felt like I could handle it.

So when we played our next game against the Hurricanes, I could barely feel my sneakers on the court.

THNK!

I felt confident. Comfortable. Cool as a banana split.

. . . the final product won't be a surprise. It'll turn out exactly the way you want.

THAK!

And man, were we cooking in that game!

SWISH!

23

We did just that. We played the second half with the same intensity as we had at tip-off.

Each one of us, every ingredient, were doing our part.

28

Congrats, man! That's so cool.

Whoa. Nice work!

In fact, I was so jazzed that I couldn't sleep that night.

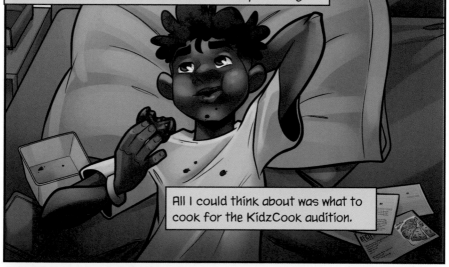

All I could think about was what to cook for the KidzCook audition.

I wondered which dish would make gramma proud.

. . . the more nervous I got.

And being nervous is never a good thing. In the kitchen or on the court. Because if you lose focus or get distracted . . .

When Rondo sent a hard chest pass to me . . .

. . . it felt like a hot knife stabbed my hand.

AGGHH!

THWACK!

My kitchen disaster led to other problems for me on the court too.

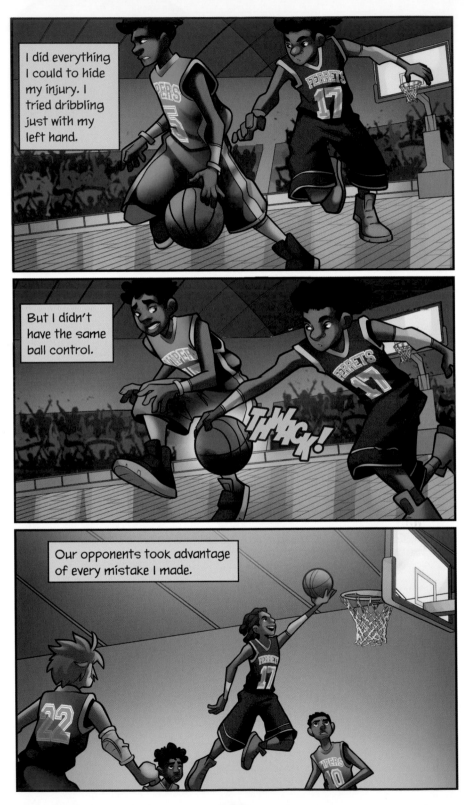

I did everything I could to hide my injury. I tried dribbling just with my left hand.

But I didn't have the same ball control.

THWACK!

Our opponents took advantage of every mistake I made.

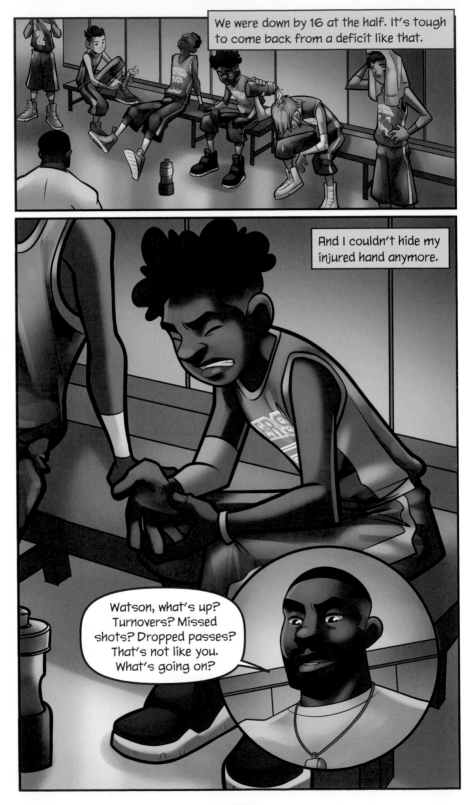

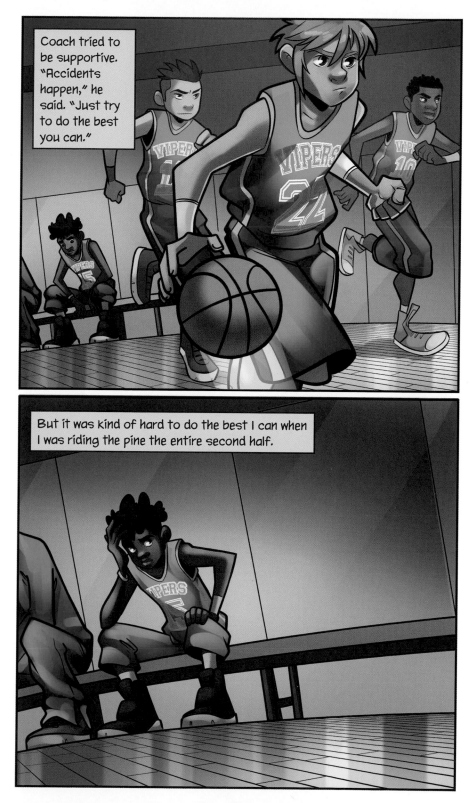

Coach tried to be supportive. "Accidents happen," he said. "Just try to do the best you can."

But it was kind of hard to do the best I can when I was riding the pine the entire second half.

SMAK!

Plus, the team couldn't seem to get in sync.

We missed many chances to get back in the game.

THAK!

51

54

But like I said. The Leopards were good. Better than any team we'd played yet.

I was still worried about the KidzCook audition too. It was just days away.

I'm open!

But I needed to focus.

If I didn't, I'd spend the game turning over the ball. And that would likely get me a well-deserved spot warming the bench again.

It was a close battle, back and forth.

But eventually, the Leopards pulled out in front.

SWISH!

Time out!

60

Charlie was our best shooter, so we got the ball into his hands.

SWISH!

He did exactly what he needed to do. We were down by two.

All they needed to do was hold onto the ball. They wanted us to us foul them, so they could shoot free throws.

THWACK!

But I snagged the ball when they made a risky pass.

There were less than ten seconds left, and I had a clear path down the court.

Okay, maybe it wasn't as clear as I thought.

So I pulled up at the three-point line. I didn't want to tie the game.

I wanted to finish it.

BZZTTT!

VISUAL QUESTIONS

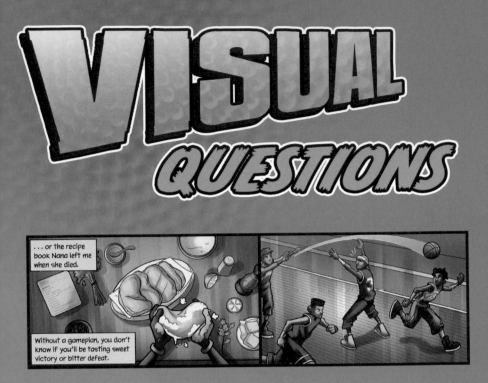

1. During the story Hank says that cooking is like playing on a basketball team. The ingredients have to work well together to be successful. Compare these two panels. How does the artist show that cooking is similar to playing with teammates on a sports team?

2. When Hank tells his team about his injured hand, Charlie becomes very upset. What visual clues does the artist use to show how he's feeling?

3. Graphic artists use facial expressions and body posture to tell us what a character is feeling. How do you think Hank feels in these panels?

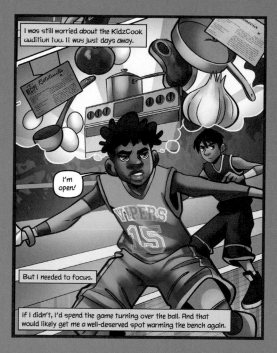

4. After Hank talks things over with his teammates, he gets back on the court. But he still has trouble focusing. How does this panel show what Hank is thinking about during the big game? What is he really focused on?

MAKE YOUR OWN
SPAGHETTI ALLA CARBONARA

Playing your best in any sport requires a lot of energy. Get yourself fueled up for the next big game with this tasty dish you can make yourself.

Ingredients

1 package spaghetti noodles
Salt
4 large eggs
8 ounces (227 grams) freshly grated Parmesan cheese
Fresh ground black pepper, to taste
10 pieces of thick-sliced bacon, coarsely chopped
2 cloves garlic, minced
Fresh chopped parsley, to taste

Directions

1. Cook spaghetti in large pot of salted boiling water according to package directions.

2. In a medium bowl, whisk together the eggs with the Parmesan cheese and pepper until well-mixed. Set aside.

3. While spaghetti is cooking, fry chopped bacon in a large skillet over medium heat until brown and slightly crispy.

4. Add minced garlic to the skillet and cook about 1 minute. Remove pan from heat.

5. Use tongs to move cooked spaghetti to the skillet. A little water from the noodles is fine.

6. Pour egg and cheese mixture over the hot noodles and stir quickly until creamy. Keep mixing with the noodles to avoid scrambling the eggs. If sauce is too thick, stir in a little of the starchy pasta water.

7. Serve pasta on plates or in a large bowl. Sprinkle with more Parmesan cheese, pepper, and chopped parsley to taste.

BASKETBALL TERMS TO KNOW

dribble — to use one hand to repeatedly bounce the ball off the floor, players must dribble the ball as they move up and down the court

fast break — a quick offensive drive to the basket, attempting to beat the defense to the other end of the court

foul — a violation of the rules, usually involving illegal contact with an opposing player

free throw — also known as a foul shot, free throws are awarded after a player is fouled by an opposing player; free throw shots are made from the foul line and are worth one point each

jump ball — a method of putting a basketball into play; the referee throws the ball into the air between two players, who jump up and try to direct it to one of their teammates

jump shot — a shot made while jumping and releasing the ball at the peak of your jump

layup — a shot made from very close to the basket, usually by bouncing the ball off the backboard

pick — to block an opposing player so a teammate can make a shot or receive a pass in open space

rebound — to catch the basketball after a shot has been missed

three-pointer — a successful shot from outside the designated arc of the three-point line on a basketball court

turnover — when a player loses possession of the ball to the opposing team

GLOSSARY

alfredo sauce (al-FREY-doh SAWSS)—a rich pasta sauce made with butter, Parmesan cheese, and cream

audition (aw-DISH-uhn)—a tryout performance to get a role in a movie or TV show

carbonara (kahr-buh-NAYR-uh)—a pasta sauce made with bacon or ham, eggs, and grated cheese

culinary (KUHL-uh-nayr-ee)—related to cooking or the kitchen

deficit (DEF-uh-sit)—an amount of points a team is behind by in a game

filet mignon (fi-LEY min-YON)—a very tender slice of beef cut from a beef tenderloin

ingredient (in-GREE-dee-uhnt)—an item that is combined with others to make something new

intensity (in-TEN-si-tee)—a quality of being intense; to do something with extra strength, force, energy, or feeling

recipe (RESS-i-pee)—a set of instructions used to prepare food, including a list of ingredients that are needed

role-playing game (ROHL-play-ing GAYM)—a game in which players pretend to be imaginary characters who go on adventures and roll dice to determine the outcome of their actions

sync (SINK)—when two or more teammates perform well together during a game or contest

ABOUT THE AUTHOR

Brandon Terrell is the author of numerous children's books, including several volumes in the Tony Hawk Live2Skate, Sports Illustrated Kids: Time Machine Magazine, and Michael Dahl Presents series. When not hunched over his laptop, Brandon enjoys watching movies and TV; reading about, watching, and playing baseball; and spending time with his wife and children at his home in Minnesota.

ABOUT THE ARTISTS

Berenice Muñiz is a graphic designer and illustrator from Monterrey, Mexico. She has done work for publicity agencies, art exhibitions, and even created her own webcomic. These days, Berenice is devoted to illustrating comics as part of the Graphikslava crew.

Jaymes Reed has operated the company Digital-CAPS: Comic Book Lettering since 2003. He has done lettering for many publishers, most notably Avatar Press. He's also the only letterer working with Inception Strategies, an Aboriginal-Australian publisher that develops social comics with public service messages for the Australian government. Jaymes is a 2012 and 2013 Shel Dorf Award Nominee.

READ THEM ALL!

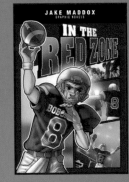

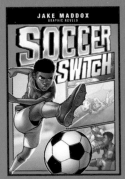